The Fishing Lesson

WRITTEN BY
Heinrich BÖLL

ADAPTED BY
Bernard FRIOT

ILLUSTRATED BY
Emile BRAVO

Eerdmans Books for Young Readers

Grand Rapids, Michigan

*I*n a small harbor on the coast,

a man in shabby clothes dozes in his tiny fishing boat.

A well-dressed tourist snaps a picture
of the peaceful scene: *click!*
And another one: *click!*
And just for good measure, one more: *click!*

The hostile sound
wakes the fisherman up . . .

The fisherman
shakes
his head.

It's a lovely
day . . .

The fisherman
nods.

But ... you're not going out to sea?

The fisherman shakes his head again.

The tourist gets more and more nervous.

Aren't you feeling well?

The tourist can no longer hold back the question that he's just bursting to ask.

The answer comes quickly:

Because I've already been out this morning.

How was the catch?

Good enough that I don't need to go out again.

The tourist climbs down into the boat.

?

I don't mean to interfere in your business, but . . .

What if you went out a second time?

Or a third?

OR EVEN . . .

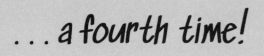

...a fourth time!

Just think about it...

The fisherman nods.

And if you go out tomorrow two, three, maybe four times again...

...do you know what would happen?

The fisherman shakes his head.

In a year or so you would be able to buy a motorboat.

In two years,
a second boat.

In three or four years, you would have a proper fishing boat.

Eventually, you would have two fishing boats, and you...

The tourist is so enthusiastic that he can't speak for a moment.

. . . you would build a warehouse!

?

A refrigerated warehouse!

And then maybe a smokehouse . . .

... and even a canning factory.

You would have your own private helicopter!

You would fly around and find all the best shoals of fish, and you'd send instructions to your boats by radio.

You would be able to buy the exclusive rights to fish for salmon...

Open a seafood restaurant...

Again, the tourist is so excited that he can't speak.

. . .

He shakes his head . . .

. . . and looks out over the waves gently rolling toward the beach, where all the fish that haven't been caught yet are happily jumping.

But that's exactly what I was doing just now. I was relaxing in my boat taking a nap until you woke me up with the annoying *click click click* of your camera!

First published in the United States in 2018 by
Eerdmans Books for Young Readers,
an imprint of Wm. B. Eerdmans Publishing Co.
2140 Oak Industrial Dr. NE, Grand Rapids, Michigan 49505
www.eerdmans.com/youngreaders

First published in the German Language as *Anekdote zur Senkung der Arbeitsmoral* by Heinrich Böll
© 1963, 1987, 1994, 2008 by Verlag Kiepenheur & Witsch GmbH & Co. KG, Cologne/Germany
Adapted and translated into French by Bernard Friot
© Editions Glénat 2012

Manufactured in China

27 26 25 24 23 22 21 20 19 18   1 2 3 4 5 6 7 8 9

ISBN 978-0-8028-5503-9

A catalog record of this book is available from the Library of Congress.